Painted Treasures

or

The Original 288 Tree Gnomes

By Donald G. Henkel
Illustrated by D.B. Henkel

Quillpen

With thanks to all who helped and with special gratitude to Jan who stands beside me with love and shared her vision and time in making this book a reality. I render a tribute to Joyce Kilmer for writing his classic poem, "Trees." *D.G.H.*

With love and thanks to Li'l "C" and L'il "D" and with hope to all the children and handicapped of the world. *D.B.H.*

First Edition 2006

Text Copyright © 2006 Donald G. Henkel
Illustrations Copyright © 2006 D.B. Henkel
ALL RIGHTS RESERVED

Published by Quillpen
Hollyhock Corners
1520 Waverly Drive
Trenton, Michigan 48183
U.S.A.

Illustrations were done in watercolor on rag board.
The body text is set in 24 point Bookman Oldstyle.
Printed and bound in Canada by Friesens of Altona, Manitoba.

1 3 5 7 9 10 8 6 4 2

ISBN-13: 978-0-9673504-1-7
ISBN-10: 0-9673504-1-7
Library of Congress Control Number: 2005904212

Here's a story in verse with a wonderful twist
Of a people that many felt did not exist.

It was all told to me in a forest one morn,
By an oddly dressed gnome,
with a paintbrush and horn.

He told me this tale from start to the end,
All in great detail so I'd comprehend.

He said he was bugler for starting their day,
Then blew his brass horn and went on his way.

You may still hear his tune
as you read what he told
And find not all treasures are silver or gold.

And so . . .

These very small folks
        that people call gnomes

Worked underground
    and there made their homes.

For years in the mine
    they had guarded the treasures.

Dark, cold and damp,
   'twas a job with few pleasures.

They grumbled and growled,
  felt they needed a move,

So a council was called
to see who would approve.

A vote was then taken
        to change their career.

When all answered yes,
there arose a great cheer!

The gnomes in the mine
        had set themselves free.

Tired of the darkness,
        they moved to a tree.

Now up in the trees
they said, "What shall we do?

It's all very nice,
and we have a good view,

But we shouldn't spend our time
just climbing and looking,

*We ought to do something
to get world-wide booking."*

Then the clever gnome, Charlie,
                spoke out from his tree.

He gave reason in rhyme,
  to which all would agree.

"When we lived underground,
        not much color was seen.

Now we've spent our whole summer
with everything green.

Although green is nice,
      too much can be dreary,

*Let's get out our paint
    and make things more cheery.*

We can make the world brighter;
   our task will be fun,

*And though we're not many
we'll paint till it's done."*

So Rachelle took the gold,
Suzanne crimson red,

Plain orange was Jake's,
mellow yellow for Jed.

The rest of the gnomes,
    made their colors to blend.

Their selection of hues
        seemed never to end.

They painted each leaf
in each tree all around;

They even painted
    the leaves on the ground.

And when they were finished—
had painted them all,

A decision was made
to do this each fall,

'cause all 'round the world,
the people could see

Painted leaves in the fall
make a beautiful tree.

Throughout the summer
you'll see now and then

Where they practice their painting
till fall comes again.

The moral is this
         and the gnomes found it true,

"If your life is unhappy,
        find new things to do."

P.S.

The Bugler Gnome
    said one more thing
I feel that you should know.

They all pack up
    and head down south
When "Winds of Winter" blow.

A Word About
The F and S Team

The Author

DONALD G. HENKEL was born in Middlebranch, Ohio, and spent most of his young adult years in Greentown, Ohio (Stark Co.). He has resided in Trenton, Michigan for the past 44 years and summers on Northern Michigan's Cheboygan River. He has three children and several grandchildren. This is his second children's book. The duo's first book, *A Legend of Santa and His Brother Fred*, has proved to be a hit with "kids" of all ages. A few of his other well-accepted works include: "The Violets are Blooming," "Down Home," "Christmas 1935," "Sentimental Treasures," and "Reminders."

The Illustrator

D.B. HENKEL was born in Canton, Ohio (Stark Co.). Studying art at the University of Wyoming and Arizona State further developed his fine natural talent. He is well-versed in all phases of art and has received numerous awards for his works in painting and sculpting. This is his second children's book.

As Joyce Kilmer so aptly states in his classic poem "Trees,"

"Poems are made by fools like me,
But only God can make a tree."

PAINTED TREASURES

or

The Original Two Hundred Eighty-Eight Tree Gnomes

Very small folks that people call gnomes
Worked underground and there made their homes.
For years in the mine they had guarded the treasures.
Dark, cold and damp, 'twas a job with few pleasures.
They grumbled and growled, felt they needed a move,
So a council was called to see who would approve.
A vote was then taken to change their career.
When all answered yes, there arose a great cheer!
The gnomes in the mine had set themselves free.
Tired of the darkness, they moved to a tree.
Now up in the trees they said, "What shall we do?
It's all very nice, and we have a good view,
But we shouldn't spend our time just climbing and looking,
We ought to do something to get world-wide booking."
Then the clever gnome, Charlie, spoke out from his tree.
He gave reason in rhyme, to which all would agree.
"When we lived underground, not much color was seen.
Now we've spent our whole summer with everything green.
Although green is nice, too much can be dreary.
Let's get out our paint and make things more cheery.
We can make the world brighter; our task will be fun
And though we're not many, we'll paint till it's done."
So Rachelle took the gold, Suzanne crimson red,
Plain orange was Jake's, mellow yellow for Jed.
The rest of the gnomes made their colors to blend.
Their selection of hues seemed never to end.
They painted each leaf in each tree all around,
They even painted the leaves on the ground.
And when they were finished—had painted them all,
A decision was made, to do this each fall,
'cause all 'round the world, the people could see
Painted leaves in the fall make a beautiful tree.
Throughout the summer you'll see now and then
Where they practice their painting till fall comes again.

The moral is this and the gnomes found it true,
If your life is unhappy, find new things to do.

Gnome (nōm) n., in fables and folklore, one of a race of very small dwarfs that live underground in caves and mines as guardians of the earth's treasures, etc.

Gnome

Tree Gnomes (trē nōms) n., a colony of gnomes, tired of their profession and living conditions underground, moved up into the trees. Painting leaves and other objects of nature became their new profession. *(According to the 2003 World Gnome Census their numbers have increased to the tens of thousands.)*

Tree Gnome

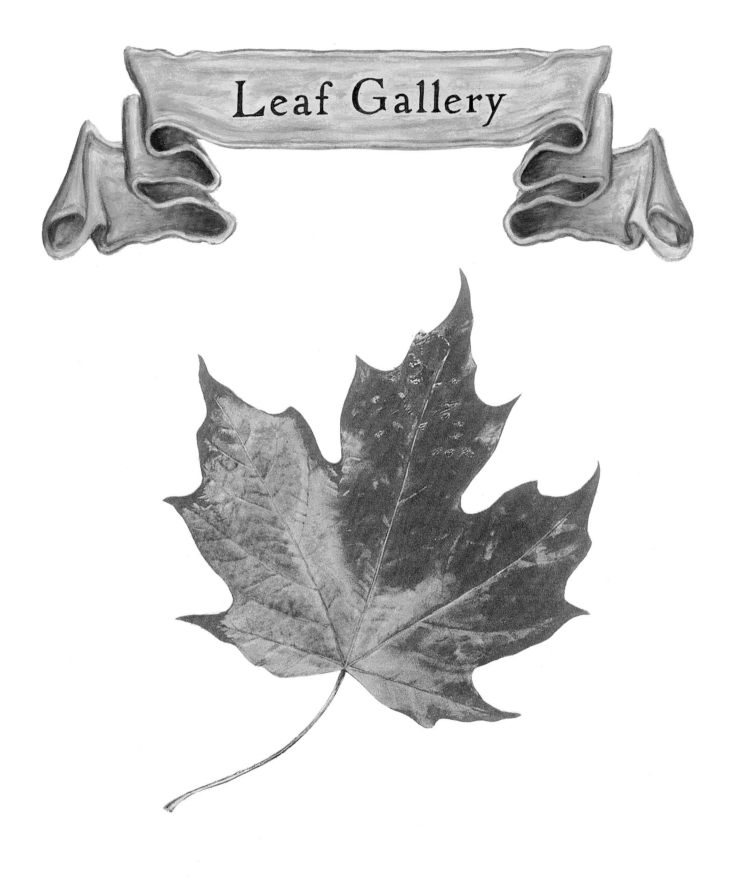

Leaf Gallery

My Leaf Collection